# The BATTLE of CABLE STREET

# TANYA LANDMAN

Barrington Stoke

First published in 2022 in Great Britain by
Barrington Stoke Ltd
18 Walker Street, Edinburgh, EH3 7LP

www.barringtonstoke.co.uk

Text © 2022 Tanya Landman
Illustrations © 2022 Sara Mulvanny

A CIP catalogue record for this book is available
from the British Library upon request

ISBN: 978-1-80090-108-7

Printed by Hussar Books, Poland

# The
# BATTLE
# of CABLE
# STREET

*To Keren,*
*for infinite wisdom and*
*expert advice*

# CHAPTER 1

## Stepney, London, 2020

There's a lot of talk these days about the Second World War and how plucky little Britain stood up to Hitler all alone. People rave about the Blitz Spirit when bombs were being dropped on us night after night and we all just kept calm and carried on. They say that Hitler's rise to power in the 1930s was Germany's problem, and that nothing like that could ever possibly happen over here.

They're talking nonsense.

But most people just want an easy life, and facts are itchy, awkward things that can make you feel sweaty and uncomfortable. If I've learned one thing in my long, long life it's that most people prefer pretty lies to ugly truths.

But maybe you're not like most people.

Maybe you're one of the brave ones?

If you are, then read on.

# CHAPTER 2

## Stepney, London, 1920s

My mother was a French dancer, according to Nathan Cohen. Nathan lived next door to us and he said Mother was as dainty and delicate as a bird. Me and my brother Mikey had to take his word for it. We didn't remember her.

Mother died a few months after I was born, leaving Father with two small children to feed and clothe. Grandma moved in to take care of me and Mikey while Father was out looking for work.

We lived in a flat with just two rooms on the third floor of a tenement block. The block was at the bottom of a dead-end road just off Cable Street in the heart of Stepney. It was a slum – the grottiest, nastiest place you could hope to imagine, crawling with rats and fleas and the like. Paragon Buildings was its official name, but the people who lived there called it the Paradise. We had one hell of a sense of humour.

The East End of London was a right old mix of people in those days. Stepney was mostly Jewish, with a big dollop of Irish thrown in for extra flavour. My family was both. Or neither, depending on how you look at it.

Grandma came from a family of Irish immigrants. Her grandparents had come to London to escape the famine in Ireland. Her parents were strict Roman Catholics, and they didn't approve of Grandma falling in love with a young Jewish man called Max. But Grandma didn't care what they thought. She married Max anyway, and after that her parents never spoke to her again.

Grandma and Max raised six sons. They were very happy together until Max dropped dead of a heart attack one morning. It seemed like a terrible tragedy at the time, Father said. But then the Great War started, and Max's death got swallowed up in a huge tidal wave of horror.

In 1914, Father and his five brothers all went marching off to fight in France. Father was the only one of Grandma's sons who came home. And if you're thinking that maybe our family was just really unlucky, you'd be wrong. Everyone in the Paradise could have told you a similar story. Me and Mikey grew up surrounded by adults who were damaged in mind or body by that bloody war. They were all haunted by the ghosts of the dead.

The Paradise was never, ever quiet. It's not surprising for tempers to flare when you pile damaged, haunted people on top of each other, pack them into a building so tight you can't stir them with a stick and keep them poor and desperate.

Morning, noon and night people shouted at each other in Irish and English and Yiddish and Russian and who knows what else. There was constant noise, and a lot of it came from the third floor where we lived. We had the Rosenbergs to the left and the Cohens to the right. Either side of them were the Smiths and the Murphys.

Mrs Smith hated Mrs Rosenberg. Their sons, Harry and Leo, had once come to blows. I can't for the life of me recall what started the fight. Who knows? Who cares? Harry Smith and Leo Rosenberg were always scrapping.

The boys made up two minutes later. But by then their mothers had got involved, taking their sons' sides and screaming at each other for hours. Mrs Smith and Mrs Rosenberg carried on arguing over the smallest things for days, weeks, years after that first falling-out. Sometimes those two women would be shouting insults all day long. They'd call each other nasty names until their throats were sore.

Every day, Grandma turfed me and Mikey out into the street to play. There was a whole gang of other kids out there, all boys apart from me. Girls living in the Paradise were Mother's Little Helpers, doing the chores, minding their younger siblings. On the rare occasions girls were allowed out, they played skipping games and the like.

But Grandma had raised six sons and no daughters. She didn't know what to do with me, so she dressed me in Mikey's old clothes. Grandma cut his hair with the kitchen scissors – short back and sides – then she did the same to me. Right up until I started school, I looked like a boy, I acted like a boy, I got treated like a boy, and that suited me fine.

Whatever game we played, our next-door neighbour Nathan Cohen was always the leader. He was three years older than me and as tall and handsome as a film star. Nathan had dark curly hair and beautiful brown eyes. He was my hero. I was half in love with him before I could even walk. And I wasn't the only one. In our own different ways, all the gang were desperate to please Nathan.

Mikey did it by making Nathan laugh. My brother had wonky legs that curved like a wishbone from hip to ankle. Mikey rolled from side to side when he walked, as if he was a sailor who wasn't used to dry land. Mikey made fun of himself to stop people making fun of him. He was always playing the fool.

Harry Smith, on the other hand, took everything deadly serious. He was a few months younger than Nathan and did everything Nathan told him to without hesitation. If Nathan said jump, Harry would only stop to ask, "How high?"

Harry was Nathan's second-in-command. When Nathan was the pirate king plundering ships for treasure, Harry was his first mate. If Nathan was a captain leading a cavalry charge, Harry was by his side yelling, "Death or Glory!" Leo Rosenberg was devoted to Nathan and would have loved to have been in Harry's shoes. Maybe that was why they fell out so often. But the rest of us never argued; we just accepted whatever roles we were handed without question.

Nathan would make up all kinds of games. Sometimes he got the ideas from films he'd seen in the cinema. But mostly Nathan pulled stories out of his head. He wrapped us up in a make-believe world that was so much more real than the dull, drab one the grown-ups lived in.

Sometimes the kids from the next street got drawn in to our games. It didn't matter what we played – we were always the goodies, and they were always the baddies. We'd fight them all day. And I mean really fight, with sticks as swords. We'd use stones as cannonballs, and anything else we could get our hands on. Nathan always seemed to walk away unscathed, but me and Mikey went home from those battles covered in cuts and bruises. I didn't know what my legs looked like without a peppering of scabs across my knees.

But our days weren't always spent yelling and running about the place. Sometimes Nathan would lead us all the way from Stepney to Bethnal Green, and on to the park. We'd lie there on the grass under the trees. Or we'd go down to the river and watch the tide coming in, filling the Thames with water. And in those quiet times my mind overflowed with tricky questions.

Why do the trees lose their leaves in winter?

Where does the water go when the tide is out?

Nathan said I asked all the right questions, but none of the answers were easy. He'd give me these long, complicated explanations. Nathan convinced me that there were fairies living in the park. The fairies made the trees lose their leaves so they could use them as blankets in winter. Nathan said there was a huge monster fast asleep and buried deep in the mud somewhere east of Tilbury. This monster breathed water instead of air and sucked the whole Thames in and out of its lungs twice a day.

The answers Nathan came up with were so good I pestered him with more and more questions. But the one thing I never, ever asked was, "Why are we poor?"

It was just the way things were. The way they always had been; the way they'd always stay. Everyone was struggling, but we were all in the same boat. The boat had so many holes in it that it was steadily sinking no matter how hard we bailed. But I never, ever wondered why.

Not until Oswald Mosley came marching into our lives, with easy answers to all the wrong questions.

It was Oswald Mosley who turned the whole bloody boat upside down.

# CHAPTER 3

## Stepney, London, 1930s

Oswald Mosley. *Sir* Oswald Mosley. He was the Sixth Baronet – whatever the hell that meant. He was an aristocrat. A toff. One of the ruling class. Later on, Oswald Mosley became the founder and leader of the British Union of Fascists and a close personal friend of Hitler.

But all that hadn't happened the first time I heard Oswald Mosley's name. That was in early 1931, when I was eight and Oswald Mosley was just an ordinary Member of Parliament.

I'd been kept home from school because I had a fever and a bad chest. Grandma was in a temper, so all day I was on eggshells. I was scared to move, trying not to let my coughing annoy her. When Mikey came back from school, I was desperate to get out and play, but Grandma wouldn't let me.

Time ticked by. At long last Father came through the door, and it was such a relief. Grandma made him a cup of tea, and as he sipped it down he read his newspaper, the *Daily Worker*. Suddenly Father said to Grandma, "Oswald Mosley's starting a new party."

"Oh?" she said.

"He's calling it the New Party," Father went on. "There's imagination for you."

I knew nothing about politics. And I suppose my head was all muddled with the fever. Images flashed into my mind of the kind of party that Nathan said posh children in books got invited to. There'd be food. Presents wrapped up in paper and string. A birthday cake with candles. Lemonade and ginger beer and the like. Jelly. Sausage rolls. Cucumber sandwiches with the crusts cut off. I'd never eaten any of those things, but it would be lovely to try.

There'd be fun and games too. Pass the parcel and musical statues, pin the tail on the donkey and blind man's buff. I'd never played any of those games, but I was looking forward to having a go. Maybe there would even be a Punch and Judy show. Oswald Mosley – the man who was starting this party – sounded wonderful.

So why did Father look so furious? Why did Grandma pinch her lips as if she'd been sucking on a lemon? I was confused.

"Mosley will be coming down here," Father said grimly. "Wanting people to join him."

"Can we?" I said.

Father turned to look at me. He was frowning as if he was struggling to understand what I'd just said.

"Will there be cake?" I asked. "And jelly?"

Suddenly Father burst out laughing.

"God bless you, Elsie!" he spluttered. Father was laughing so hard his eyes were watering. Grandma joined in. And it should have been nice to see the pair of them looking happy for once. But being laughed at like that made me want to cry. I sweated hot and cold all over, not understanding why what I'd said was so funny. I had no idea who Oswald Mosley was, but I truly hated him for making me feel so stupid.

It took a few minutes for Father to steady himself. But when he did, he explained that Oswald Mosley wasn't having that kind of party. He was a politician. A Member of Parliament.

Oh, I thought. One of *them*. They came from a whole different world to us. I'd seen Members of Parliament on the rare occasions we could afford to go to the cinema. There had been newsreels of posh old men in top hats and black suits. Their shirts had collars starched so tight they looked like they could choke a man.

"Members of Parliament?" Father used to say. "What do they know? What do they care?"

Suddenly I felt deflated.

Grandma called Mosley a few nasty names, so I realised he wasn't the kind of politician she'd want to vote for.

"The man can't decide which side he's on," Father said. "Tory one minute, Labour the next. And now a party all of his own."

"It won't last," Grandma said. "Oswald Mosley will see which way the crowd is heading, then walk out in front claiming he's their leader. He'll promise everything and deliver nothing but hot air."

They carried on talking, Grandma and Father. I didn't listen. It was grown-ups' stuff – nothing to do with me.

That was the first time I heard Oswald Mosley's name. But it wasn't the last. And every time someone mentioned him, I felt that same hot flush of embarrassment I'd had when Father and Grandma almost wet themselves laughing at me.

You know how sometimes you notice something for the first time? Maybe a lamp post or a drinking fountain or a statue. It's always been right there in plain view, but somehow you've missed it before. But then you do suddenly see it. And after that it smacks you right between the eyes every time you go past it. You can't stop seeing the thing.

It was like that with Oswald Mosley. One day I'd never heard of him. The next his name seemed to be on everyone's lips.

# CHAPTER 4

I might not have heard of Oswald Mosley before
that day, but I most certainly knew who Ted
Lewis was. There wasn't a soul in the East End
of London who hadn't heard of him.

His real name was Gershon Mendeloff, but
everyone called him The Kid, or Kid Lewis. He
had been a world champion boxer back in his
day. The Kid was Father's age or thereabouts.
But while Father and his brothers had every
kind of bad luck thrown at them, Fortune had
smiled on Kid Lewis. He had toured the world
as a young man, winning fights, mixing with

film stars and the like. He'd lived the kind of life I couldn't even begin to imagine.

The Kid had made himself a fortune, and then he'd spent it all, bit by bit. His fame had sent him up like a shooting star, and then he'd fallen back down to earth again. The Kid had come home to London a while back and was now broke and looking for work.

You'd see The Kid sometimes in the street, and there would always be a crowd gathered around him. Men laughing and joking and clapping him on the back. Women smiling and flirting. Children trying to get close in the hope that some of The Kid's star quality would rub off on them.

One morning, Nathan managed to get The Kid's autograph. I remember Nathan coming back to the Paradise that afternoon, his face all flushed like he had a fever. He gathered the gang around him, saying he had something to show us.

I thought maybe Nathan had caught one of those fairies who made the leaves fall off the trees in the park. I was expecting something amazing and held my breath so long I almost fainted. And then all Nathan pulled from his pocket was a torn scrap of paper with a scribbled signature across the middle.  Mikey reached out to take it, but Nathan slapped his hand away.

"No touching," Nathan said, like the paper was made of stardust.  "This is The Kid's autograph."

There was this long silence while Nathan stared at the piece of paper.  The rest of us just stood there confused, not really getting it.  I had no idea what an autograph was, but I was thinking if it was The Kid's, then maybe Nathan should give it back?

"What is it?" said Davey, the youngest of the Rosenberg lads.

Nathan gave us all a disgusted look.  Then he folded the piece of paper very neatly and tucked it back inside his pocket.

\*

Ted "Kid" Lewis was a nice man.  Everybody loved him.  Right up until the day he got a job as Oswald Mosley's bodyguard.

The first I heard about it was when me and Mikey came back from school.  We always went to the flat for a slice of bread and margarine before heading out to play. If there was no bread at home, we'd try the Jacobsons' bakery in Cable Street. It was a place of magical wonders. The smells that wafted out of the door made me and Mikey drool like dogs every time we walked past.

The bread and cakes marked the passing of time better than any calendar. Challah was a sweet plaited bread that appeared every Friday morning for Shabbat. Honey cake was made for Rosh Hashanah, the Jewish new year. Triangles of hamantaschen, filled with poppy seeds, were for the festival of Purim in the spring. Me and Mikey could never afford to buy nothing, but Mrs Jacobson had a soft spot for my brother. She'd sometimes slip him a little something if she had anything to spare.

We were coming up the stairs to the third floor of the Paradise that day when we heard Mrs Smith and Mrs Rosenberg on the landing yelling at each other. There was nothing strange about that, but then we heard Mrs Cohen joining in. And there was that name again. Oswald Mosley.

*Mosley this* and *Mosley that*. The three of them were kicking the name back and forth at each other like a football.

"Gershon Mendeloff's his bodyguard, ain't he?" said Mrs Smith. She spat The Kid's proper name out like it was a filthy swear word. "And he's as Jewish as you are. I'm telling you, Mosley ain't no antisemite."

Mikey and I stopped dead. Our mouths dropped open. Antisemite? I felt a cold prickle of horror. It didn't matter if you were Jewish or not. If you grew up in Stepney, you'd heard of antisemitism. You knew it meant hate and fear and every kind of bad thing you could possibly imagine. Most of the people in the Paradise were first-, second-, third-generation Jewish migrants who'd been driven out of their homes by antisemitism.

Back then I didn't know the history. I didn't know the Russian Tsar had been murdered in 1881 and people had used that as an excuse to have a go at innocent Jews. I didn't know the attacks that followed were called pogroms or that there had been so many of them over the next few years. But I did know that Max, my grandfather, had watched his village burn because of antisemitism. I did know he was the only member of his family who managed to get out of Russia after their home was destroyed. He was just a little lad who made that long, terrifying journey all by himself. Max was the lucky one who lived to tell the tale.

Mrs Rosenberg called Mrs Smith something I ain't repeating. Then she said, "The Kid's been in one too many fights. He's had all the sense knocked out of him. No one in their right mind would work for Mosley."

"The Kid's a fool," agreed Mrs Cohen. "He's being used."

"No he ain't!" said Mrs Smith. "If Gershon Mendeloff thinks Mosley's all right, then that's good enough for me. You lot see antisemitism everywhere."

"Because it *is* everywhere!" Mrs Cohen yelled.

Then Mrs Rosenberg said, "I'm looking at it right now." Her voice had gone very low and clear and cold, as if she'd spat the words right into Mrs Smith's face.

Mrs Smith didn't answer. She must have gone inside, because we heard the door slam.

Mrs Cohen called after her, "Who in the hell does a toff like Mosley need defending from anyway?"

And then Nathan was coming down the stairs with a face like thunder. There was a small scrap of paper in his hand. As he came towards us, he started tearing it up.

"Coming out?" Nathan said, and there was a catch in his voice as if he was holding back tears. It was so unlike Nathan that me and Mikey forgot about going upstairs for a slice of bread and margarine. Without a word, we turned and followed him.

When we got into the street, Nathan stopped for a moment. His jaw was clenched tight like he was fighting hard not to cry. He took a deep breath. Steadied himself. Then Nathan opened his hand and let the wind snatch all those tiny fragments of paper away.

Even now, all these years later, I can see Nathan standing there with that terrible, sad look on his face. His eyes were shiny with unshed tears as he watched that precious autograph disappearing with the wind. It's strange how some things stick in your mind. Maybe if you can't make sense of them at the time, they hang around in your head until you can understand.

Looking back, I think that was the moment when Nathan started to grow up. Until then, things had been simple. People were either good or bad, right or wrong, hero or villain. There wasn't anything in between. Nathan had thought Kid Lewis could do no wrong. And yet now Nathan's hero had done something awful. Nathan was confused. Hurt. And I hated The Kid for that even more than I hated Oswald Mosley.

# CHAPTER 5

Life carried on. We went to school. We played in the street. But things had shifted, just a bit. I didn't know what was bothering me, but I had this constant niggling sense of unease. It was like being a long way from home and suddenly starting to want the toilet. It was like feeling scared that maybe I wouldn't get to a bog in time.

Nathan was still our leader and we still ran wild, but somehow the games had changed. When we battled the kids from the next street, Nathan wasn't pretending any more. He was practising.

I could see something was preying on his mind, eating away at him, but I didn't have the words to ask what it was. And I'm not sure Nathan could have explained it anyway. But it was like there was a dark cloud hanging over his head which coloured everything.

Then we heard The Kid was helping set up some sort of a club with a man who used to be the England rugby captain. The club was called the Biff Boys, and they were training up young lads to help keep order at Oswald Mosley's New Party meetings. Mikey said it sounded like something out of a comic. He started dancing around, punching the air, like he was in a boxing ring.

"Wham! Splat! Bam! Biff!" Mikey said, hitting imaginary villains. "Come on, lads, let's biff those baddies!"

Mikey tried to joke Nathan out of his mood, but nothing worked. So in the end, Mikey stopped.

After that, we all tried to avoid the subject of Kid Lewis and Oswald Mosley and the Biff Boys. But there was no getting away from it.

*

There was a general election later that year, a few months after I'd turned nine. And general elections always got people talking down our way. On every street corner, there were communists and anarchists and socialists all yelling out their opinions and all coming up with different ideas about how to make the world a better place. It was always noisy.

But then Oswald Mosley put up Kid Lewis to stand in the election as a New Party candidate for Stepney. The third floor of the Paradise almost exploded with the arguments that raged back and forth.

Mikey and me tried to keep our heads down and stay out of the rows: it was grown-ups' business. But Nathan kept fretting about it, saying over and over, "What the hell does The Kid think he's doing?"

All we could do was shake our heads and look blank. "Dunno," we replied.

Nathan got more and more fed up with us, and my niggling sense of unease just grew and grew until I could barely stand still.

Kid Lewis was a Jewish celebrity, a world champion boxer, a hero. The Kid standing for election in a Jewish area like Stepney?  Oswald Mosley must have thought his man would win easily.

In the Paradise, Mrs Smith was right behind Kid Lewis, but most of the other grown-ups seemed to think that The Kid was wasting his time.

The night before the vote I remember Father saying to Grandma, "He's a lovely man, but The Kid ain't no politician."

I remember wanting to tell Nathan that, but I was scared to in case it upset him again.

Father was right.  In the end, Kid Lewis only got 154 votes.  It was a laughable result, people said.  It was embarrassing not only for The Kid but for Oswald Mosley and the New Party.

*Thank heavens for that*, I thought.  *The Kid can go back to being Nathan's hero.  And we won't ever have to hear Oswald Mosley's name again. Nathan will cheer up now.  That's the end of it.*

But I was wrong.  It was only the beginning.

# CHAPTER 6

In the spring of 1932, the number of unemployed people in Britain reached a whole new peak. Those days were dark and desperate for the likes of us. The East End of London was suffering, but so was the rest of the country. There were marches, with hundreds of skinny men walking all the way from Glasgow to London, trying to make their voices heard.

With no work, there was no money. With no money, there was no food. Men who'd fought in the Great War had been promised a land fit for heroes when they came home. And now

they were having to watch their children starve. But it didn't matter how loud they shouted as they marched. The posh politicians, the men in smart suits, the toffs who ran the country couldn't seem to hear them.

But Mosley was listening. And planning. Wondering how he could make use of all that anger and desperation. He went off to Germany to pick the brains of Hitler's mates. He went to Italy to cosy up to Mussolini. Mosley came back with a head full of new ideas.

That summer a member of the New Party was up in court for producing leaflets saying that all Jews ought to be kicked out of the country. The man got convicted, and that should have been the end of it. The New Party should have made it very clear that they didn't like what he'd done, kicked him out of the party and moved on. But they didn't.

The New Party sat on the fence. They said they didn't *approve* of the leaflets, but they didn't *disapprove* either. They said they had no opinion at all. They swore blind they had no official answer to what they called the "Jewish Question".

*And what was the Jewish Question?* I hear
you cry.

I asked Nathan about it. And he gave me a
long, complicated answer. It was so contradictory
and made so little sense I thought he was joking.

"Jews are bankers who control the world,
Elsie," Nathan said. "Didn't you know? We're
not really poor. The whole of Stepney's just
pretending. But we're also communists, who want
to overthrow the whole capitalist system. You
didn't know we were planning to do that, did you?
Jews all want to marry Christians and corrupt
the blood of native Britons. We're hell-bent on
destroying the English. Oh – but we also keep
ourselves to ourselves and don't mix. Funny that.
We're warmongers, you know. Always busting
for a battle. We bloody love it! Oh, but we're also
cowards who refuse to fight for our country. My
father? Leo's father? Both of them fighting in the
Great War? Their brothers who died? That must
all have been a lie. They made it up. They were
sitting at home for four years, plotting to take
over the world."

I thought Nathan was making it up, like he
did with the fairies and the leaves in the park,
and the monster that breathed in the Thames.

I almost laughed, but then I saw that look in his eyes. Anger. Hurt. Confusion. And my niggling sense of unease became a tearing pain in my chest.

I didn't understand what was going on, but it was impossible not to know that something ugly was coming. It was just lapping at our toes at the moment, but creeping up, inch by inch, like an incoming tide.

Mosley was doing exactly what Grandma had predicted he would. He was testing the water. Biding his time. Watching the crowd to see where it was heading before leaping out in front and declaring himself their leader.

# CHAPTER 7

Grandma was also right about Mosley's New Party not lasting. The 1931 general election was a disaster for him. Whatever his strategy had been wasn't working, so he looked to Hitler for inspiration.

Hitler, who did have an official answer to the Jewish Question.

In the autumn of 1932, Mosley made some changes. The New Party became the British Union of Fascists, commonly known as the BUF.

The Biff Boys became Blackshirts.

Groups of them dressed in dark uniforms and jackboots started hanging around on street corners. They didn't do much, not to begin with. But there was something about the way those Blackshirts looked at you when you went by that sent shivers up your spine. It was like they thought they were better than everyone else. Like the rest of us were dirty or stupid. Like they were powerful and we were weak. The Blackshirts would stare at Mikey's wonky wishbone legs and whisper things to each other.

Mikey laughed at everything and kept telling me that they were just a bunch of boy scouts in fancy dress. Big kids playing soldiers. But every time Mikey told me that, he said it long after we'd gone past them and very quietly, so that only I could hear. When he laughed about them, he never ever did it to their faces.

When the New Party became the BUF, Kid Lewis stuck with Mosley. And more and more grown-ups talked about it, pursing their lips, shaking their heads, agreeing that The Kid must have had a screw knocked loose in the boxing ring.

Things got more and more unsettling. Mikey could tell me not to worry until he was blue in the face, but I couldn't shake off the feeling that the ugly tide that had been lapping at my toes was now sloshing around my ankles.

It was small incidents to begin with. Yelling and shouting. Scuffles in the street. Rubbish bins emptied over doorsteps. The kind of thing that happens from time to time when people are crammed together like rats in a barrel. The kind of thing that might be explained away as a silly tiff, a small rivalry, a row over something and nothing.

"Stop fretting, Elsie," Mikey said when I told him my worries. "Things like that happen all the time."

And it was true. There had always been all kinds of arguments going on in the Paradise and down along Cable Street. Catfights when factory girls finished a shift and came spilling along the pavements. Brawls when Irish dockers were turned out of the pub at closing time. That all still went on. But on top of that there were incidents that Mikey kept brushing off as "little things" that meant nothing. Then one day Nathan lost his temper and grabbed the front of Mikey's jumper. He put his face right up to my brother's and said, "Open your eyes, Mikey. Ain't you noticed? All these 'little things' you think are nothing? They're only happening to Jewish people."

About a week after that, Leo had another fight with Harry. Only this time it wasn't about something and nothing. This time it was because Harry had called Leo a "Jew boy". He was just teasing, Harry said later. Didn't Leo have a sense of humour? It was a joke! But Leo hit him so hard Harry was seeing stars for days.

And then late one Saturday night, a few drunken louts walked up Cable Street throwing stones at shop windows. One cracked the glass door of the Jacobsons' bakery. As soon as we heard about it, me and Mikey went round to see if they needed help clearing up, because the Jacobsons were almost family.

Eva Jacobson, the couple's only child, had been engaged to Albert, Father's youngest brother, during the war. The day before the war ended, Albert got a letter telling him that Eva had died from the influenza.

It must have seemed to Albert like it was all the wrong way around. Soldiers in the trenches weren't supposed to get bad news. It was the people at home who were meant to do the worrying and the grieving.

Albert's commanding officer wrote to Grandma and said Albert had taken Eva's death badly. Albert was killed by a sniper's bullet later that same day. But whether Albert had been careless or whether he'd been unlucky, the officer didn't say.

The Jacobsons must have missed Eva something terrible. Her and the grandchildren she might have given them. Grief made some people bitter and hard. But it made Mrs Jacobson kind. She had a warm smile and a huge heart.

"It's nothing," Mrs Jacobson told us when me and Mikey arrived at the bakery. "Cracked, not broken. Just drunken louts."

But I'd got to an age when I could see through her reassurances. Mrs Jacobson was trying not to frighten us because we were children. She wanted to protect us. And maybe Mikey was too scared to face the truth, because he believed what she said. I was tired of Mikey telling me not to worry, so I didn't say anything. But I'd noticed on the way up Cable Street that all the shops with Irish names over the doors had been left untouched.

Even Kid Lewis finally noticed what was happening. One day a rumour went around that he'd had a massive falling-out with Mosley. The Kid had marched into Mosley's office and demanded to know if the man was an antisemite. And whatever answer Mosley had given didn't satisfy The Kid. The world champion boxer thumped Mosley right there in his office, knocking him out cold. And, for good measure, The Kid did the same to the bodyguards who were supposed to be protecting Mosley.

The story whipped around the Paradise like a tornado. Everyone on the third-floor landing spilled out of their flats. Everyone but the Smiths. There was whooping and cheering like something out of one of those jolly Hollywood musicals. *Any second now*, I thought, *we're all going to burst into song*.

But Nathan didn't join in. All he said was, "The Kid should have killed Mosley while he had the chance."

# CHAPTER 8

In life, there are worries that worm their way into your mind and stay there. In the great, grand scheme of things, they're not really important. But they grow bigger and bigger in your head until you ain't got room to think about nothing else.

I was aware of what was happening with Oswald Mosley. I knew Hitler was on the rise in Germany. Nathan said that Mosley was heading down the same path. I should have been scared witless, but all that suddenly faded into the background. Because in 1933, Nathan Cohen

turned fourteen, and my whole world flipped upside down.

Time is a funny thing when you're a child. The grown-up world was so far removed from mine it might as well have been filled with aliens. Real life to me was out on the streets running wild with Nathan and Mikey and Leo and Harry and the others. It never occurred to me that it wouldn't last for ever. I never thought that any of us would get any older.

And then there came this one day when everything began to change. It was a beautiful sunny winter's morning, crisp and clear and cold. Instead of mucking about in the streets near the Paradise, Nathan led the gang all the way to the park. He was the pirate king, and we were his crew. It was like old times.

Nathan was in a wonderful mood and laughing at everything Mikey said. Leo and Harry were getting on, and Leo's little brothers, Davey and Joe, were as happy as pigs in muck. Kid Lewis and Mosley seemed a million miles away.

"Let's do knights on horses," Nathan said when we got to the park. "We'll have a jousting match."

He looked at me, and my heart gave a tiny flip. "I'll be your trusty steed, Sir Elsie."

So I got on up Nathan's shoulders. Mikey got on Harry's, and Davey was on Leo's. Joe was the referee. We took it in turns to charge at each other. We didn't have weapons, so the riders clenched our right fists, held our arms out straight and tried to thump our opponent as our horses galloped past each other. It started off sensibly, but it wasn't long before we were having a three-way battle. Riders tried to pull each other off their horses, and horses kicked each other's shins. Joe kept screaming, "Foul!" while all of us ignored him and laughed and yelled our heads off. Until the park keeper came and told us to shut up.

After that, we sat by the pond. Leo and Harry got the idea of kneeling right by the side and seeing if they could catch the ducks. And Leo managed to touch one, but then it flew at his face and gave him such a fright he fell in.

It was a lovely day. We stayed there right until it started to get dark and the streetlights were lit. When we walked home, Joe, Davey and Mikey were ahead. Leo and Harry had started scrapping about something, so Nathan fell into step beside me.

We didn't say much. We didn't need to. It was nice. Comfy. When we reached the third floor of the Paradise, I said to Nathan, "See you tomorrow."

"You won't," he said. "I've got to go and talk to my uncle. I'm starting work soon, Elsie."

I must have known deep down that it had to be coming soon, but I'd shut my eyes to it.

Nathan Cohen would have his last day of school on his birthday. The same thing happened to every child who grew up in the Paradise. It was perfectly normal, but it happening to Nathan seemed to me to be the most terrible tragedy.

Nathan was clever. And I mean really clever. If he'd been born forty or fifty years later, he could have done anything he wanted to. But staying on at school or going to university was never an option for him. It was never an option for anyone in the Paradise. You might have been a genius – an Einstein or a Shakespeare. But once the hands on your life clock were pointing to fourteen, that was it.

It was like metamorphosis but backwards. You transformed from butterfly to caterpillar overnight. Suddenly you weren't a child. You were an earner. A worker. No more games in the street. No more pretending to be a pirate king, or a cowboy riding the open range. No more wild flights of the imagination. You were just a slug from now on who had to earn your keep, pay your way, contribute to the family budget.

Nathan got a job working for his uncle who had a tailor's shop on the Mile End Road. After Nathan started work, we hardly saw him. When we did, he didn't want to come out and play. He was striding ahead into the dull, drab, grey world of grown-ups, leaving his gang far behind.

And me?

Heartbroken.

# CHAPTER 9

The rest of our gang tried to stay in the make-believe world, but Nathan was the glue that had held us together. Without him, everything began to slide. Harry tried to fill Nathan's shoes, but all he did was re-run the games that Nathan had dreamed up. Nathan wasn't there to add fresh twists or think up new ideas, and it felt more and more like we were just going through the motions.

For weeks, we were like lost souls. Our gang didn't know what to do with ourselves. Then there was this one wet Sunday when the

weather was as dismal as we all felt. Grandma was up to her elbows with laundry, and Father was sleeping. He'd had some work that week up at the fish market, and he was worn out.

Staying inside and getting under Grandma's feet wasn't an option. Me and Mikey joined the gang, but we were looking sideways at each other like we were strangers, not knowing what to do or say.

Our gang wandered around for a while, drifting west until we passed Tower Bridge. The wind howled up the river, and the city streets were deserted. The whole place looked bleak and miserable.

Mikey, being Mikey, made a joke of it. There was a drinking fountain at the side of the road, and he stopped beside it.

"Let's play polar explorers," Mikey said. "I'll be the whale."

And he lowered his head, took a mouthful of water and then blew it out in a spout that hit Harry in the face.

Mikey hadn't meant to. There was no nastiness in it. I thought it was funny, so I started to laugh. And that set Leo and his brothers off, and Harry was always touchy about anything Leo did.

Harry thumped Leo, catching him under the ribs, winding him. Leo's little brothers went for Harry while Leo was bent double, gasping for breath and clinging on to Mikey for support. Joe jumped on Harry's back, and Davey started kicking his shins.

But they were too small to make any impression. Harry gave them a few thumps and it was over.

And maybe they'd have made up in the end, like they always did. But then Harry called Leo a Jew boy again, and this time he wasn't even pretending it was a joke.

I thought Leo would lay Harry out flat, but Leo just stood there, staring. Harry walked off on his own. Without a word, Leo and his brothers stood up and headed in the opposite direction. Me and Mikey were left alone.

*Sticks and stones may break my bones, but names will never hurt me.*

You'll have heard that saying, I expect. We used to chant it in the school playground. What a load of rubbish! Names are like the blades of knives: they cut deep and leave scars. Names hurt because they're meant to.

Leo's and Harry's mothers soon heard about the fight, but they didn't wade in to defend their sons. Mrs Smith didn't argue with Mrs Rosenberg. But she didn't apologise for Harry's behaviour. Mrs Smith just ignored Mrs Rosenberg as if the woman didn't exist. And the silence between them was a whole lot more scary than all the shouting had ever been.

# CHAPTER 10

I was missing Nathan something awful. I was upset that our gang had fallen apart. And all the time I was busy fretting over that, Mosley kept pushing things here, nudging them there, seeing how far he could go. And the more he pushed, and the more he nudged, the further Mosley got.

He stopped saying that the BUF didn't have any opinion on the Jewish Question. Hitler had come to power by stirring up antisemitism – why shouldn't Mosley do the same? The ugly thoughts about Jews that people had once kept to themselves got said in public. Quietly at

first. But then louder. And louder. Until people were shouting at the tops of their voices. And the more people shouted, the uglier those thoughts got.

Most people in our neighbourhood had no time for Mosley and the BUF. Jewish or Irish, we'd all been on the receiving end of his kind of talk before. It didn't matter if you were born in this country or not. The reason your parents or your grandparents had fled their homeland and washed up in London didn't matter – nor what horrors they'd left behind. There were always people somewhere muttering about immigrants and wanting to keep Britain for the British.

Like I said, Nathan was clever. He didn't plan on working for his uncle for ever; he was determined to improve himself. Nathan carried on his education at night classes. He read every book on the shelves of Whitechapel Library. Nathan knew all sorts of things, and he said there was no such thing as a native Briton.

I remember Nathan telling me, "Everyone on this island came here from somewhere else. It just depends how far back you go along their family tree."

People in Stepney would have been likely to agree with him. But just across the road in Bethnal Green and in Hackney and Bow and other boroughs beyond there were plenty of people who considered themselves native Brits. They were ready and willing to hear what Mosley had to say.

When I was young, the Cohens' Friday-night dinners had always been loud, happy affairs. I'd hear Nathan and his older brothers laughing and joking with their parents through the walls. About once a month, Nathan's aunts and uncles and cousins would come along too. But there were too many of them to fit into that tiny flat, so they'd spill out onto the landing, and me and Mikey would get caught up in it.

But Friday evenings now weren't like they had been. The Cohens' talk had got serious. There were earnest, angry, worried conversations about what was going on and what they should do.

The older Cohens were in favour of keeping their heads down, keeping quiet. By behaving well they'd prove that Jews were law-abiding citizens who were a help not a hindrance to the country. It was the only way to tackle antisemites, Nathan's mother and father and uncles and aunts said.

But Nathan and his brothers and cousins said their parents had been behaving well all their lives and it hadn't made the blindest bit of difference. What was needed now was to fight fire with fire. They all joined the Young Communist League and went to meetings after work and at weekends.

*

After our gang had fallen apart, me and Mikey had started going up the park together on Sundays. We'd do stupid stuff like sitting on the grass watching the clouds change shape, making pictures of them.

"That one's an elephant," I'd say.

"No it ain't! It's a crocodile," Mikey would reply. "Hey, look at that one there, Elsie. Looks like Grandma on a bad day."

Sometimes we'd race each other, weaving between the trees. Other times we'd just sit and watch the ducks.

But then there was this one spring day when me and Mikey noticed a couple of things on the walk to the park that me feel hot and cold all over.

There was a boarding-house sign advertising ROOMS AVAILABLE.

But scribbled underneath were the words: *No Irish. No dogs. No Jews.*

A little further on was a corner shop that had a notice saying ASSISTANT NEEDED and then: *Only British-born Christians need apply.*

Mikey tried laughing it off, but by the time we got to the park we were both uneasy. A few people were hanging about near the bandstand, and we thought maybe a concert was going to start. The idea of hearing a few tunes cheered us up no end.

"Care to dance, my lady?" Mikey said to me in a crisp, posh voice.

"Why yes, kind sir," I replied in the same accent. "That would be most delightful."

Mikey took my hand and together we pranced across the grass.

But when we got to the bandstand we saw the people were Blackshirts starting a BUF rally. A crowd was already gathering to listen.

"Load of codswallop!" said Mikey. But he said it in a low voice and took my hand, dragging me away towards the gates. "Let's go get a pie, Elsie. Who the hell wants to hear any of that?"

When we reached the gates, I looked back. Codswallop or not, that crowd by the bandstand just kept on getting bigger.

# CHAPTER 11

There were always sheets of newspaper on the back of the toilet door of the Paradise. The *Jewish Chronicle* or the *Daily Worker*, torn into squares, hanging on a nail for you to wipe your backside with. I'd read bits and pieces when I was sitting there, doing my business – if there wasn't anyone outside, banging on the door demanding their turn on the bog.

One January morning in 1934 there was a copy of the *Daily Mail* hanging there. Right away I felt something was wrong. People in the Paradise were either socialist or communist,

which is why they read the *Daily Worker*. The *Daily Mail* was a right-wing rag, Nathan said, full of lies. Nobody round here would touch it. So how had that thing got here?

I didn't even want to wipe my backside with it. I started to pull bits of paper off the nail until I could find some sheets of the *Daily Worker*. But then the headline on one torn square of the *Daily Mail* caught my eye: "Hurrah for the ..."

*Hurrah for the what?* I thought. Hurrah for the king? Hurrah for the Prime Minister? Hurrah for the weather? What was there to cheer about?

I pulled off another square. Turned it over. And there was the rest of the headline.

"Hurrah for the Blackshirts!"

You know how sometimes you can't resist picking at a scab or squeezing a spot? You know you shouldn't, but somehow you can't help it. It was like that then. I knew I shouldn't be reading the *Daily Mail*, I knew it would leave me feeling grubby, but I couldn't stop myself. I found all the bits of the article underneath the headline, put them together and read the whole thing.

It was written by Viscount Rothermere, the owner of the *Daily Mail*. Since Nathan had joined the Young Communists, I'd heard him cursing Viscount Rothermere often enough. The Viscount was stinking rich. He'd inherited houses and land and a title. And power. He was what they call "a pillar of the Establishment".

"What are these Blackshirts," Viscount Rothermere asked in the article, "who hold 500 meetings a week throughout the country and whose uniform has become so familiar a feature of our political life?"

Five hundred meetings a week? Right across the country? That sent another cold shiver down my spine. I thought the Blackshirts were just in Bethnal Green!

"They fall mainly into two distinct age-groups," Viscount Rothermere went on. "One consists of those who were just old enough to take part in the war, and have been discouraged and disgusted by the incompetence of their elders in dealing with the depression that has followed on it. The other is made up of men too young to remember the war but ready to put all their ardour and energy at the service of a cause which offers them a vigorous and constructive policy in place of the drift and indecision of the old political parties."

Viscount Rothermere went on to say that carrying on as we were wasn't an option.

Well, Nathan would have agreed with him on that one. I often heard Nathan telling his parents that the whole political system needed ripping up and starting over.

Yet somehow I didn't think Nathan Cohen's and Viscount Rothermere's plans for a golden future would look the same.

"Hurrah for the Blackshirts," Viscount Rothermere said again towards the end of his article. "They are a sign that something is stirring among the youth of Britain." Then he wrote about patriotic pride and how the youth of today would shape the future.

It was baffling. Viscount Rothermere made it all sound exciting. Almost. And yet there was something sinister about it. All the talk of British youth and of British patriotism sounded all right. Sort of. Father had fought for his country, hadn't he? So had Mr Cohen and Mr Rosenberg. There was nothing wrong with being patriotic. And yet I could feel this sense of unease squirming in my guts.

I was eleven, so it was nothing I could explain, not even to myself. I didn't have the words for it. But, looking back, I can see that deep down I'd realised there was something being said in that *Daily Mail* article that wasn't being said out loud. It was a hidden message that was clear to anyone who wanted to read between the lines.

When Viscount Rothermere said "British", it didn't include me and Mikey, and it most certainly didn't include Nathan. It didn't matter if your family had been settled here for generations. You didn't count if you were Jewish, if you were Irish or half-French, if your skin was the wrong colour or your face didn't fit. If you were different in any way at all, then you weren't part of the British club.

And there was something else bothering me. Two hazy questions were trying to take shape in my mind that I couldn't put into words until years later.

The first was about Mosley.

He was a toff – a posh boy who'd been to a public school. A man of money and property –

one of the ruling class.  And everyone from down our way knew from bitter experience that the ruling class liked to hang on to its wealth and privileges.  So why was Mosley promising working people right across the country that he'd tear down the whole system?  Why was he saying he'd turn the world on its head so they could have a better future?

The other question was about Viscount Rothermere, who couldn't have been a more rock-solid pillar of the Establishment if he'd been carved out of marble.  He wouldn't want things to get better or easier for working people, not if it meant giving up any of his money or power. Yet here was Viscount Rothermere cheering on Mosley and his bully-boy Blackshirts.  Why? What was he getting out of it?

# CHAPTER 12

A few weeks later, Mikey came back from the toilet with some pieces of newspaper in his hand and a wicked grin on his face. He nodded at me, winked and jerked his head towards the door. I knew that meant Mikey didn't want Grandma hearing what he had to say, so as soon as I got the chance I went out and joined him on the landing.

"Look, Elsie!" Mikey said, and he was pointing to the newspaper. It was announcing a competition. There was going to be a big rally of the BUF, and it was the kind of thing you

could only get into if you were a party member. But the newspaper had got hold of 500 tickets and was offering them as prizes in its competition. All you had to do was write a letter explaining "Why I Love the Blackshirts".

"You going to help me, Elsie?" Mikey said. "Your handwriting is nicer than mine."

"You're kidding, ain't you?" I said.

"No, I ain't," he replied. And his eyes were glinting like he was really excited.

For a moment, the ground seemed unsteady under my feet. *Not Mikey*, I thought. *He can't have been sucked in by Mosley, can he?* In that split second, anything seemed possible.

Mikey must have seen how scared I looked because he said, "What do you take me for? I just thought we could have a laugh entering the competition. They all take themselves so serious. They need the mickey taking out of them."

It was such a relief that Mikey was kidding, and it had been so long since me and him had a good giggle, I went along with it. I suppose I wasn't thinking straight.

We wrote the most ridiculous, overblown letter, full of praise and enthusiasm for Mr Mosley.  Me and Mikey egged each other on, getting more and more outrageous with every sentence until I was laughing so much I could hardly hold the pen.

We said how we worshipped the very ground Mosley walked on.  That we were ready and willing to lay down our lives for the future of Britain and our Empire under Mosley's great and glorious leadership.  His order, his discipline, his vision had made us strong and given us hope and courage.  We couldn't wait to do our bit to serve.

The letter was daft.  It was so clearly making fun of the whole stupid lot of them I didn't think any more of it.

But blow me down, flattery really can get you everywhere.  Two weeks later, the day after my twelfth birthday, Mikey called me out to the landing again for another quiet word.  He'd met the postman coming up the stairs and taken a letter addressed to the pair of us before Grandma and Father could see it.

"Present," Mikey said, handing the letter to me.

We'd won tickets to the rally.

I was all for throwing them straight down the toilet, but Mikey had a better idea.

"We'll go along," Mikey said. "How about we heckle, eh? We'll tell Mr Mosley exactly what we think of him."

# CHAPTER 13

## Olympia, 7 June 1934

The BUF rally was being held at Olympia. I'd never been so far from home in my life, and I was terrified, truth be told. On the way there, I kept telling myself the jittering in my stomach was excitement. We were on an adventure, just me and Mikey playing a little joke, having a bit of a laugh.

When we got there, the place was swarming with people. I'd never seen so many in one place. A lot of the crowd who'd come to hear Mosley

were working people in worn-out clothes. But there were neatly dressed women too, on the arms of men in dark suits who all looked well off. And there were some real toffs in their evening clothes. Men with bow ties and top hats, and women in silks and furs, dripping with jewellery.

There was a huge crowd of protesters as well, carrying placards, yelling slogans. Communists, anarchists, socialists, anti-fascists. They were all herded together by a bunch of police on horseback who were holding batons and looked ready and willing to use them.

Suddenly me and Mikey's little joke didn't seem so funny any more.

We should have been with the protestors, I thought. Adding our voices to theirs. But we were already stuck in the crowd of people who were going in, and it was like being carried along by the tide – there was no getting out of it.

Inside, everything felt unreal. It was like me and Mikey had wandered onto a film set. The place looked just like one of those rallies that we'd seen on the cinema newsreels. In Italy with Mussolini. In Germany with Hitler. Those events had seemed so foreign and so far away. And yet here we were at the same thing, only this was happening in London.

All around us people were wide eyed and fresh faced, bursting with excitement about the prospect of seeing Mosley, their hero, in the flesh. They were pushing and shoving to get the best seats. There was a bloody great band playing stirring patriotic marches to get people in the mood. You couldn't hear yourself think. Maybe that was the whole point.

Union Jacks were everywhere, as well as the BUF's black-and-yellow flag. And all the time me and Mikey were trying to find a place to sit, there were arc lamps flicking beams of light around the place like at the start of a 20th Century Fox film. One lamp swung around as we were making our way up the aisle and dazzled the pair of us. I stumbled into Mikey and almost knocked him off his feet. And then I felt a hand on my arm and – hell's teeth! – a Blackshirt had got hold of me. I was suddenly so scared I wanted the toilet.

He knew, I thought. The Blackshirt knew that me and Mikey were there because we'd lied. He knew we'd cheated in that competition, that we'd been making fun of them and didn't belong here. All the whispers I'd heard about what Blackshirts did to people they didn't like flooded into my head and washed the sense out of my ears.

I didn't realise I'd shut my eyes until I heard a voice, close to my face, shouting, "Elsie! You all right?"

And when I opened my eyes, there was the Blackshirt, and he still had his hand on my arm. But I saw now that it wasn't just any old Blackshirt. It was Harry Smith.

Harry Smith, who'd been Nathan's right-hand man. He nodded at me and Mikey and then jerked his head sideways towards a pair of seats just down the row.

"Those are free," Harry said, giving us a sharp look. "Sit there. Good to see you both here."

He gave us another smart nod, then stood to attention again.

I looked at Mikey, and Mikey looked at me. And like puppets on strings we walked to the seats that Harry had pointed out. Now I not only needed the toilet, I felt sick to my stomach.

I don't know what was worse. Seeing Harry in that uniform or letting him think we were here because we were fans of Oswald Mosley. Mikey had gone pale, and I knew he was regretting our joke just as much as I was.

"We shouldn't have come," I said to Mikey. "We shouldn't be here."

I don't suppose he could hear me over the noise the band was making, but he got the sense of it.

"Don't you worry, Elsie," Mikey yelled, giving my hand a squeeze. "Things will be fine, you'll see."

But things weren't fine. Things were so far from fine they could have been in Australia.

There's something strange about a crowd. People aren't individuals any more. Minds, hearts, thoughts, feelings – they all get swallowed up. A crowd is one great blob that can be steered in any direction the leader wants it to go. I could already feel it happening, and it was starting to choke me.

*

Mosley was more than half an hour late starting. Maybe it was because of the protestors outside.

Or maybe Mosley just liked to keep people hanging around because it made him feel more powerful.

When he did come in, he made his entrance like he was God Almighty. I've never seen anyone who was so in love with himself. The lights of the hall dimmed, and the arc lamps all swung round to light the stage. The band struck up another march, and there was a fanfare as Mosley appeared. Beside him were six bodyguards carrying more Union Jacks and more BUF flags.

The crowds' cheering almost burst my eardrums. And the arms raised in fascist salutes behind me nearly knocked my head off.

But the moment Mosley started speaking, I started listening. I stopped being scared, and I started getting angry.

I didn't understand everything I heard and saw that night, not at the time. But there at Olympia an answer began to take shape in my mind. An answer to one of the hazy questions that had come into my head when I'd been sitting on the toilet reading the *Daily Mail*.

I still didn't have a clue about why Viscount Rothermere was backing Mosley. But I began to see why Mosley was promising to tear down the whole system so working people could have a better future.

It was because Mosley was drunk. Not on beer or strong whisky. On power. Standing in front of crowds who worshipped him had made him feel like a god. He couldn't get enough of their attention. Mosley didn't give a damn about the greater good that he was talking about. All those promises of his were just empty words. Hot air. This was all for him. He would promise people anything – anything at all – as long as they kept on cheering him. Mosley was wallowing in their adoration like a pig in muck. And the crowd was drunk too; they weren't thinking straight. This was mass hysteria.

To begin with, I couldn't really follow everything Mosley said. He was going on about Britain for the British and global conspiracies with Jewish bankers holding the whole world to ransom. His sentences were long and complicated. He used big words that were hard to understand. And the sound system was so dreadful I couldn't properly hear half of it. But as he went on, somehow I could *feel* what he was saying. I could grasp his meaning from the tone of his voice, from the way he stood and the way he moved his hands. Bit by bit, his speech seemed to translate itself into something that I could understand.

Mosley was smiling on that crowd. He didn't use these words, but he was telling them, *I'm your friend. Your best, your only friend. I'm going to take proper care of you.* It was like he was putting an arm around their shoulders, reassuring them, saying, *It's all going to be fine.* He was offering them sympathy and understanding.

*Things are bad, are they? No work? Low wages? Hungry kiddies? Can't pay the rent? That's so unfair! You deserve better. You're talented, you are. You should have a bright, shining, golden future. What a mess, eh? But it ain't your fault. None of it is your doing. You've been let down. All those other politicians have failed you, but I won't.*

*We all know who's to blame for the state the country's in, don't we, my friends? We know whose fault this mess is! None of it is our doing, is it? We're not at fault.* **They** *are.* **They're** *the guilty ones.* **They're** *the ones who stole our jobs, our homes, our future. Well, we ain't having it*

*no more, are we?  We ain't going to stand for it.*
***They're** going to pay for what they've done to us.*

*I'm on your side*, Mosley was telling that crowd.  *We're in this together, ain't we?  Things will be fine for you.  They will be fine for all of **Us**. Just as soon as we get rid of **Them**.*

Mosley had an easy answer to everyone's problems: blame **Them**.

Blame the Jews.

# CHAPTER 14

I don't know how long Mosley had been speaking for when Mikey and me discovered we weren't the only people who'd got into that rally under false pretences.

It felt like we'd been trapped in there forever when Mosley paused for breath and someone on the tiered seating behind and above us started booing. Just one person, that was all.

But those horrible arc lamps swung around, lighting up the place where the shout had come from. Blackshirts who'd been standing

to attention in the aisles were suddenly scrambling over chairs and people to get to whoever had booed. We couldn't see much, but we could hear it. Screams. Thumps. Groans. And then all that was drowned out by the people around us chanting, "We want Mosley!"

It took a few minutes for the noise to die down and for Mosley to start up again. When he did, someone else began heckling down at the front. It was a young woman this time, lit up by the arc lamps, but the Blackshirts didn't care if she was female. They piled into her, hitting her so hard they must have broken her nose. I could see the blood even from where I was sitting. They forced her arms behind her back and started dragging her out of the hall.

And the worst thing? The worst thing was that Mosley's supporters didn't lift a finger to help her. They just clapped and cheered and waited for him to start up again.

And Mosley did. He promised that he would make Britain great again, then stopped to draw breath. There was a second of silence. And at that moment a single leaflet fluttered from the ceiling down to the stage.

The leaflet fell slowly. Ten thousand people watched it twirling through the air. It landed gently on the ground at Mosley's feet, and someone yelled from above.

"Down with fascism!"

I couldn't see who'd shouted. But I knew that voice.

"Oh my god," I said.

Me and Mikey looked at each other. Together we said, "Nathan!"

All the eyes that had been on that leaflet flicked upwards. A man was balanced right up in the iron rafters, lit by those horrible arc lamps. We were too far away to see his face, but it was Nathan all right. He was standing tall, just the way he did when he was being the pirate king. But he wasn't fighting the kids from the next street now. And he didn't have us backing him. Nathan started climbing across the rafters to get to safety, but from each corner of the roof Blackshirts appeared.

Mosley carried on speaking, but no one was listening to him no more. Everyone was watching a dozen of his thugs chase one man up in the roof. Chaos was breaking out beneath. People were trying to get out of the way in case one of the thugs fell. The Blackshirts were closing in on Nathan, and I just couldn't help myself.

"You bleeding bastards!" I yelled. "Leave him alone!"

I don't suppose for a minute that Nathan heard me, but the Blackshirts in the aisle did. I watched Nathan swing himself upwards onto the next level. There must have been some sort of platform up there because Nathan was running now.

After that, I couldn't see what was happening. Because one of those lights had swung round and was blinding me.

Then there was a crash of glass and a thud as if someone had fallen to the floor.

*Nathan!* My heart was screaming. *Nathan! Nathan!*

But Mikey had my hand and was pulling me out of my seat and we were running. Because the Blackshirts were after us now. Mikey and me.

# CHAPTER 15

It didn't matter that I was a twelve-year-old girl. It didn't matter that Mikey was thirteen and had wonky legs and couldn't run fast enough to get away from them. The Blackshirts laid into us with fists and then feet. And if one of them was Harry Smith, I couldn't tell. There were so many, and I was in such pain. I'd wanted to go to the toilet since we'd got in there, and I couldn't control it no more.

I wet myself. Twelve years old and I wet myself. I thought the shame of it would kill me.

But it was just as well I had.

I don't know how much more damage those Blackshirts would have done to the pair of us if I hadn't wet my pants. They wanted blood as much as Mosley wanted power. They might have killed us. But the sight and the smell of my urine made the Blackshirts stop beating us up. They walked away back to the rally laughing, leaving us in the lobby of Olympia.

Me and Mikey sat there for a while, too shocked to move, looking at the protestors outside. And at the police, who must have seen what was happening to me and my brother but who hadn't lifted a finger to help us.

My eyes were swollen and my head ached. My nose was bleeding and I felt like my ribs were cracked. I was sitting in a soaking-wet dress. And Mikey hadn't fared much better. We looked at each other, too upset to cry. We managed to get to our feet and stagger outside. Somehow we got past the crowds of police and protestors and wandered along the pavement, dazed and bloody. And it was then that a cabbie spotted us and said, "In there, were you?"

Me and Mikey nodded, and the cabbie said, "Blackshirts do that?"

We nodded again, and he pointed to his cab and said, "Hop in."

"We ain't got no money for the fare, mister," said Mikey.

But that cabbie didn't want paying. He was a communist, he said. And anyone who was prepared to stand up to Mosley was a friend of his.

I'd never been in a taxi before. In normal times, I'd have loved it. But I was miserable, standing there in my soiled dress. I was so terrified that I'd stain the cab's upholstery, I didn't want to get in.

It was like the cabbie read my thoughts.

"I've had worse messes in the back of my cab, believe me," he said. "Toffs on a night out? You wouldn't believe the kinds of things they leave in there."

Me and Mikey could hardly say a word, but the cabbie was a talker and he kept up a steady stream of chat. He said that Mosley had arranged with the Metropolitan Police for his Blackshirts to keep order inside the building. That's why the police just stood there and watched me and Mikey getting beaten up.

"Dangerous man," said the cabbie. "Mosley thinks he's above the law. And the police are just letting him get away with it."

I didn't really follow the rest of what he said. I was too busy thinking about Nathan – that crash of glass, that thud … I was imagining Nathan maybe dead or lying in hospital somewhere.

And once more the cabbie seemed to be reading my thoughts. "You got someone at home who can fix up your cuts and bruises?" he asked. "Because you don't want to go to hospital, not if you can help it. The police are going through the hospitals, taking the names of anyone injured. They'll charge protestors with disturbing the peace, but not them fascist thugs. Free country? You've got be joking!"

The cabbie drove us all the way back to the Paradise.

When we got home, Grandma made us a cup of tea and told us we were fools, thinking we could mess with Mosley. Father said we were a pair of idiots, but he was glad we were home safe.

It was only then that Mikey and me burst into tears.

# CHAPTER 16

Nathan got back home unscathed about two hours after me and Mikey did. I started crying again with sheer relief. Nathan had managed to get out of the building and lose himself among the protestors. He didn't have a mark on him, but that was Nathan for you. He was invincible.

Then much later Harry Smith finally showed his face ...

And there was one hell of a row on the third-floor landing that night. The whole of the Paradise heard it. The whole of London, probably.

Harry Smith had found himself a leader in Oswald Mosley who was bigger and older and more powerful than Nathan Cohen. And it didn't matter what anyone said. Harry Smith's loyalty to Mosley was as solid as rock.

Oh, the Cohens and the Rosenbergs and the Murphys all had their say. Father and Grandma waded in. They all tried to reason Harry out of it. But it wasn't reason that had got Harry into the Blackshirts.

His family backed him up. They were British, they said. It was time to stand up for their rights. They spouted a whole load of disgusting nonsense, and there was no changing any of their minds.

The Smiths moved out of the Paradise not long after. None of us knew where they went. And we didn't care. I can't say anyone was sorry to see the back of them. The atmosphere on the third-floor landing had grown so thick you could cut it with a knife.

We got new neighbours. A family who'd fled from Germany with just the clothes on their backs moved into the Smiths' flat. They arrived pale and shocked. I could hear them from the landing sometimes, fretting and crying. I didn't

understand German, but I didn't need to.  One
look at them was all it took to know that they
were worried sick for the friends and relatives
they'd left behind.  And scared stiff that the thing
they'd run from was starting up here.

*

Going to the rally at Olympia changed me and
Mikey.  We weren't the same people we had
been before.  The smile had been wiped off my
brother's face by fascist fists.  Mikey couldn't find
a funny side to anything for a long time.  And I
didn't just feel bruised in my body, I felt bruised in
my head.  Like I'd never be able to think straight
again.  I was so angry I didn't know what to do
with myself.

Before we went to that rally, we'd both
thought deep down that everything would turn
out all right in the end.  We'd learned it from
films, I suppose.  The hero would always triumph
by the time the credits rolled, no matter how bad
things got, no matter how many deadly perils he
faced.  The baddies lost; the goodies won.  That
was the way things were meant to be.

Yet now it was plain even to Mikey that the baddies were on the rise, and we weren't at all sure that the goodies would beat them.

Olympia was a turning point in all sorts of ways. The violence had been so bad that the true nature of the BUF couldn't be hidden any more. So many people had been beaten up and so many people had witnessed it. Mosley's mask was off, and everyone could see the ugliness of what lay beneath.

There were no more hurrahs for the Blackshirts on the front pages of the *Daily Mail*. Viscount Rothermere withdrew his support from them. Some said he was disgusted by what had happened at Olympia. But others said that the Viscount was worried about losing the newspaper's advertising revenue. Who knows? The man certainly carried on admiring Hitler, so maybe his change of mind had more to do with money than his conscience.

A lot of people tore up their BUF membership cards after Olympia. But a lot of people didn't. And a lot of others joined the BUF for the first time. And those new members were scarier than the old ones because they couldn't be excused on the grounds they didn't understand the threat that Mosley posed.

They understood all right. Violence and antisemitism were exactly what they signed up for.

And so for the next two years things just got worse and worse. Me and Mikey might have wanted to stick our heads in the sand and pretend it wasn't happening, but Nathan wouldn't let us.

"Come with me," Nathan said one evening. So we did. Me, Mikey, Leo and all his brothers, following Nathan like we used to. Only this time he didn't lead us up the park or down the river. Nathan led us along the road to a hall where the Young Communist League were having a meeting.

That night, the communists finally answered the question of why Viscount Rothermere had been cheering on the Blackshirts.

It was all part of a con trick, the communists said, played on the very poor by the very rich. Toffs like Viscount Rothermere and Mosley con one group of poor, desperate people into believing that their equally poor, equally desperate neighbours are to blame for their suffering.

They might use different words, but what they were really saying was: *Hungry are you? Cold? Miserable? It's not us bosses and landlords and toffs who are to blame! We're not exploiting you! Of course we're not hogging all the money and land and power to ourselves! Oh no. No, no, no. The reason you're hungry is because of those people next door. They're the ones who are stealing the food out of your kiddies' mouths. They're taking your jobs and your houses. That's why you're cold and miserable. They're the ones you need to get rid of.*

The communists said that toffs split working people into **Us** and **Them**. Then they set the two groups at each other's throats. As long as we were fighting among ourselves, we didn't look up to see who was really pulling our strings. And while we were busy tearing each other to pieces, the toffs could stay exactly where they were, sitting on the fortunes they'd inherited from their parents and would pass on to their children. Living nice and comfy without any of them ever having to do a hard day's work.

Now I ain't saying that the communists were perfect. Over the years it's sometimes felt like people on the political left are our own worst enemies. But back then it seemed to me that the communists were asking all the right questions. *Why are we poor? What can we do about it?*

None of the answers were easy. If we wanted a better, fairer world and a brighter future, it was going to take hard work, courage and sacrifice. There would be pain and suffering, and it would be one hell of a struggle. But it could be done, the communists said. The way things were, the ways things had always been, was not the way things had to remain.

At that very first meeting I discovered something stronger than fear and anger.

I discovered the possibility of change.
I discovered hope.

# CHAPTER 17

A watched pot never boils, so they say. It ain't
true. For two years, everyone in Stepney watched
Mosley heating things up to boiling point. He
opened BUF branches in Bethnal Green and Bow,
Shoreditch and Limehouse. It wasn't safe to be
out on the streets alone any more, not if you
were a communist, and especially not if you were
Jewish. Gangs of Blackshirts roamed around,
their knuckle dusters at the ready. Anyone
they didn't like the look of would be treated
the same as me and Mikey had been at Olympia.
But at least the Blackshirts were a noisy lot.

Most of the time you could hear their jackboots coming down the road a mile off and head the other way fast.

What I found more frightening were the fascist sympathisers. The ones that went to BUF rallies in plain clothes to cheer Mosley on. I'd walk along the street or stand in a shop queue and never know if the person next to me was one of *them*. It got so I didn't want to talk to strangers for fear of what might come out of their mouths.

By the autumn of 1936, that watched pot was not only boiling but about to bubble over.

Me and Mikey had both started work by then. Him in the Jacobsons' bakery and me in the dressmaker's shop next door to it. I spent my days stitching buttonholes and adjusting hems. Real life happened before and after work, and at weekends when Mikey and me and Nathan and the others were with the Young Communists.

1936 was one hell of a year. It started with the death of the old king. It ended with the abdication of the new one. But seeing as the new king had been cosying up to Hitler, I can't say he was much missed down our way.

In 1936, General Franco, another fascist dictator, joined Hitler and Mussolini on the world stage. General Franco started up a bloody civil war in Spain. Terrible, terrible things were happening over there, and what was our government doing about it?

Nothing.

They pretended it wasn't happening. Hoped that if they kept their heads down and their mouths shut, it would all go away.

Well, we weren't having that. The members of the Young Communist League rolled up their sleeves and organised a big rally in Hyde Park for Sunday, 4 October. But about a week before it, Nathan burst in to a meeting with a poster in his hand. He'd ripped it off the wall on his way back from work and spread it out on the table, his hands shaking.

"Look," Nathan said. "Look."

The poster advertised a BUF march and rally on the very same day we were supposed to be having our big event in Hyde Park.

But this time Mosley wasn't going to Olympia or any of them posh places up west. He was coming right into the East End.  The poster said Mosley was going to parade his fascist thugs along the "Jew-ridden and communistic" streets of Aldgate and Whitechapel.

A chill of horror went right through me.

Mosley was coming here, to find the beating heart of Stepney and rip it out.

*

Mosley's march was meant to provoke us.  He wanted us angry.  He wanted us scared.  He wanted violence.

So what should we do about it?

Ignore it, a lot of older people said.  Mosley was trying to bait us, trying to start a fight that would only make us look bad.  They said the best thing to do was rise above it.  Everyone should just go inside, shut their doors, bar their windows and wait for it to pass.

Tempting.  Very tempting.

But the *Jewish Chronicle* ran an article saying the government should ban Mosley's march.  The Jewish People's Council Against Fascism and

Antisemitism said the same. They organised a petition and got 100,000 signatures in a matter of days. The local MP and four borough mayors asked the Home Secretary to stop Mosley setting foot in the East End.

It didn't make the blindest bit of difference.

The Home Secretary said a ban would be undemocratic and the march must go ahead. He said Mosley had a right to free speech. And it seemed that Mosley's right to free speech was far more important than our right not to be threatened in our own homes. The message from the Home Secretary was loud and clear: Mosley was a toff, and we were nothing. We should button our lips and keep quiet.

Which only left one option.

Mikey asked, "What are we going to do, Nathan?"

Nathan looked at me and I looked at Nathan and together we said, "We're going to stop him."

# CHAPTER 18

### Sunday, 4 October 1936

The week leading up to Mosley's march was mayhem. Communists, socialists and anarchists were out all hours of the day and night. The whole gang apart from Harry Smith were in the thick of it – me and Mikey, Nathan and Leo, Joe and Davey. We stuck up posters, handed out leaflets, chalked slogans on walls.

*Mosley's provoking civil war!*

*No Hitler torture here!*

*Stop the fascist hooligans!*

Vans were going around with loudspeakers blaring out messages that told people what was going on and what they should do. The air was filled with anger and excitement. Day by day it cranked up and up until, come Sunday morning, it was at screaming pitch.

We knew Mosley's lot were gathering at Tower Hill in the morning. They'd lined up on Royal Mint Street to get inspected by him before the march moved off at 2 p.m. Four groups were heading to four different meeting points in Bethnal Green, Limehouse, Bow and Hoxton. We didn't know the exact route they were planning to take, but Gardiners Corner was the gateway to the East End – the big junction where five roads met. They were bound to go through there.

But if there were enough protestors blocking the way, Mosley might just try heading along Cable Street. Windows and doors were being boarded up when me and Mikey left the Paradise. And barricades were being put up a hundred yards apart, right down the length of the street. Irish dockers, Jewish tailors, Somali sailors – all sorts of men and their wives and children were hauling out old furniture and packing cases and anything else they could get their hands on.

They were shifting, stacking, blocking the street so no fascists could leak through.

Father had gone out early with Mr Cohen and Mr Rosenberg. They were all marching with the Ex-Serviceman's Movement Against Fascism that morning, parading along the streets to show people how they felt about Mosley.

Nathan, me, Mikey, Leo and his brothers were all meant to be marching with the Young Communists.

But it didn't work out the way we'd planned.

So what happened that day?

We had to piece it together afterwards. We'd been in different places, seen different things. There were a thousand and one different dramas playing out in the East End streets that day.

But let's start with Father's, shall we? Because it was what happened to him and Mr Cohen and Mr Rosenberg and their comrades that really set the tone.

There they were, marching along Whitechapel Road with heads held high, medals pinned to their chests, carrying the British Legion flag. They were all old soldiers who'd fought for their country, and who'd watched their brothers-in-arms suffer and die. They'd seen horrors most of us couldn't even begin to imagine. All those men were heroes who'd been promised everything and given nothing.

They were nearing Gardiners Corner when they were stopped by the police and told they couldn't go any further. Well, they weren't having that.

"This is our borough!" they shouted.

"We live here!" they pointed out.

"If Mosley's allowed to march, then why the hell can't we?" they asked.

But the police had their orders from the Home Secretary. The old soldiers were told to go home.

It didn't take long for tempers to flare. And the police thought the best way to deal with a group of old soldiers was to charge their horses at them. Horses carrying police with batons, who swung at the heads of unarmed men.

You can't treat people like that and not have trouble. There was a right old battle, but men on foot can't do much against men on horses. The police managed to get hold of the British Legion flag, tear it to shreds and smash the pole.

Nice, eh? Very respectful. That was what maintaining law and order looked like down our way.

Word about it spread like wildfire. It was an outrage! People who'd planned to stay indoors and keep their heads down now spilled from their homes to join the crowd.

There was chaos and confusion, a great crush of people that were pouring into the streets, and we couldn't make it to where we were supposed to go. Me and Mikey lost sight of Leo and his brothers. Nathan was with us to begin with. But then I saw he had this gleam in his eye. Before I could ask him what he was up to, he'd slipped off.

We found out later that Nathan wanted to be at the heart of things. He was out to fight the fascists, not the police, even if there didn't seem to be much difference between the two that day. Nathan managed to work his way down to Royal Mint Street. He was right there in the front line of the battle. Of course he was. Where else was the man who'd been in the rafters at Olympia going to be?

It was Nathan who heard the fascists shouting filthy antisemitic slogans and threats, and yelling, "*M-O-S-L-E-Y! We want Mosley.*"

It was Nathan who got the crowd of protestors shouting back, "*So do we. Dead or alive.*"

Nathan was there when the fighting broke out. And this time he didn't survive unscathed. This time Nathan got two teeth knocked out. This time he got his skull cracked.

By a police baton? Or a fascist fist? He couldn't remember afterwards.

Nathan fell. And he was bloody lucky that the men around managed to drag him to one of our first-aid posts. If he'd ended up in hospital, the police would surely have arrested him. Nathan would have ended up in court like a lot of other protestors did.

But we didn't know what was happening to Nathan at the time. Me and Mikey were hanging on to each other's hands the way we had when we were small. We were getting washed along with the vast tide that was flowing towards Gardiners Corner.

Leo and Joe and Davey were way ahead of us by then. They got themselves in the fast bit of the flowing crowd and were carried right into the middle of the junction. They could see the trams that had been driven down the road and then abandoned by their drivers to make a blockade. Leo said you could tell in one glance that there was no way the fascists were going to get through there. But the police just weren't giving up. They were acting like Blackshirt bully boys, Leo said.

From where we were, me and Mikey couldn't see a thing. We could hear the noise, that was all.

Shouting.

*"They shall not pass!"*

*"Down with fascism."*

Repeated over and over.

Police whistles screeched; horses' hooves pounded. There were cheers and boos. Boos and cheers. And screams. Screams.

Leo and his brothers managed to get themselves up onto a lamp post and were hanging on for dear life. They could see the police horses charging again and again at the ordinary men and women who were risking horrible injuries to stop Mosley getting his way. Leo and Joe and Davey yelled themselves hoarse with each charge: "*Stand firm! Hold tight!*"

And with each retreat they shouted: "*Oh, well done! You're bleeding marvellous, you lot!*"

As for me and Mikey ... I started to get the feeling that we were in the wrong place. It was plain as day that no one was getting past the crowd at Gardiners Corner. I had a prickling of the hairs on the back of my neck and a gut feeling in my stomach.

We had to get back to Cable Street.

"We've got to get out of here, Mikey!" I said.

He gave me a look. "How?"

It was true. We were hemmed in. Pressed together like sardines in a tin. But then Mikey smiled at me and winked.

"I'm going to be sick!" he said loudly. He clapped his hands over his mouth and made a gagging noise.

And it's amazing how even the tightest of crowds will melt apart if people think they might get splattered with someone else's vomit.

Me and Mikey got ourselves to Cable Street by cutting along the back lanes, ducking down alleyways and climbing over walls that we knew from all those years of playing with Nathan and the gang. And it felt exciting, like it had when we'd fought the kids from the next street.

But then we heard the noise, getting louder the closer we got. It was the same noise we'd heard at Gardiners Corner only this time it seemed ten times louder.

But we were nearly there. We were nearly safe. We shot out into Cable Street like bullets from the barrel of a gun and skidded to a halt.

That morning, when we'd left for Gardiners Corner, there had been a barricade going up on Cable Street at least ten yards to the right of the lane we'd just come down. But the police had smashed it up while we'd been ducking and diving our way back. A lorry had been overturned to make a second barricade about eighty yards to the left. Irish dockers with crowbars were in front of it, standing beside Orthodox Jews and Somali sailors, all yelling their heads off.

"*They shall not pass! They shall not pass! They shall not pass!*"

Fifty yards to our right, me and Mikey saw the police preparing to charge.

"Oh my bloody Christ!" Mikey said. He looked like he really was going to be sick now. He'd gone deathly pale.

The order was given. The police were coming. And we were in their way.

Maybe we should have turned around and gone back up the lane. But mounted coppers would likely have followed us and smashed our heads in. There was no way that we could outrun a galloping horse. As it was, the sight of those mounted police made me and Mikey freeze.

A scream was rising in my chest, but my throat was too tight to let it out. Which was probably a good thing. Because then I heard someone yelling, "Get up there, quick!"

There was a woman leaning out of an upstairs window ten yards to the right of us. She was pointing to the shop directly across the street from me and Mikey. There was a ledge above its front door that we'd be able to stand on.

But the horses were coming now. Hoof beats pounded the paving. Crossing the street was like running through treacle. We couldn't move fast enough.

But blow me down, someone was coming out of the woman's house and running *towards* the horses. A little kid. Six? Seven? A boy with a bag of marbles. What in the hell did he think he was doing?

The woman – his mother? – was screaming her head off.

"Jakey! You get back here!"

And Jakey did what he was told. But first he scattered those marbles across the road.

"Shift yourselves!" he screamed at me and Mikey.

We didn't need telling twice. I gave Mikey a leg up. He scrambled onto the ledge, then hung on to the drainpipe and reached down to pull me up after him. But I didn't feel any safer up there. We might not get crushed underfoot, but those police batons could still reach us.

"Bloody hell, Mikey!" I screamed. "We're going to die!"

But the police riding in the front of the charge must have seen what Jakey had done. They were trying to rein their horses in. But the ones behind were still coming forward. And suddenly the horses were piling on top of each other, snorting and squealing in panic. Their riders were yelling, and the horses were treading on the marbles. Slipping, sliding, falling.

There was the horrible sound of horseshoes grating across stone. A bleeding great horse came thudding to the ground, slamming sideways into the shop door beneath us. The rider flew from the saddle, and the policeman's helmet went skidding across the road. Hooves thrashed while other horses bucked and reared and slid every which way, inches from our feet. The horse below us struggled and heaved itself back up. Its rider lay groaning on the street.

The police retreated, carrying the injured rider with them. And Jakey darted out again, grabbed the helmet that was still lying on the road and made off with it as a trophy.

# CHAPTER 19

Later that afternoon the Police Commissioner told Sir Oswald Mosley that they'd tried their best, but they just couldn't clear a way through for him. The Blackshirts had to turn their little fascist backsides around and march along the Embankment.

And that night we had ourselves a party. It seemed like the whole of the East End was joined together in one almighty celebration. Father came along with Grandma. She'd kept herself busy that day in the flat above the bakery, hurling out milk bottles alongside Mr and

Mrs Jacobson.  She'd even emptied chamber pots on the heads of the police who were trying to break their way through.

Poor old Nathan was bruised and bloody and his head was aching, but he staggered along with Leo and Joe and Davey and Mikey and me to celebrate in the park.  Nathan even managed to dance with me when the band struck up. When the music stopped, he kissed me.  On the forehead.  Just a quick dry peck.  As if I was his sister.

Let me tell you something about that day. There were 3,000 fascists at Royal Mint Street in their uniforms, ready to march.  Six thousand foot police had been sent to clear the way for them as well as the whole of the mounted division.

But there were hundreds of thousands of ordinary East Enders, the people who gathered at Gardiners Corner and in Leman Street and Cable Street, who all turned out to do the right thing. Hundreds of thousands who risked life and limb to hold back those bleeding fascists.  Hundreds of thousands of good men and women and children who didn't believe Mosley's lies.  They didn't believe their neighbour was their enemy; they could see things straight, as they really were.

I was young and full of hope, burning with a passion to make the world a better place. I knew this fight wasn't over, even as me and Mikey were dancing across the grass in the park. I'd seen Mosley with my own eyes, seen the madness in his face, heard the madness in his voice. Madmen don't give up easy.

Of course, I didn't know back then how bad things would get. Our fight with fascism had hardly begun. It wasn't over for a long, long time and it cost us all so very, very much. But that's a story for another day.

There are some jobs that should just stay done. Once you defeat an evil like fascism, that should be the end of it. It took me years to realise that it's like housework. No matter how often you clean up, the dirt just keeps on coming back.

But on that one day in October 1936, hundreds of thousands of decent people had won.

The police said, *Yes. Of course, Mr Mosley. You can march through the East End.*

And the Home Secretary said, *Why, yes. Freedom of speech and all that.*

His Majesty's Government said, *Oh yes. Free speech. Frightfully important.*

And Mosley himself declared that he was a toff and he could do whatever he bloody well pleased.

But we said, *No. No, Mr Mosley. You can't. These are our streets. This is our home. What we say matters. And we say No.*

And our NO was louder than all their yesses.

We stopped them.

They

Did

Not

Pass.

# AUTHOR'S NOTE

Many years ago, when I was still at school, I spent some time volunteering at a soup kitchen in Cable Street. It was there that I first heard about the events of Sunday, 4 October 1936, when the residents of Stepney stood shoulder to shoulder to prevent fascists marching through their home.

It was an inspiring story, but it was also a confusing one. I'd "done" Hitler's rise to power in 1930s Germany as part of my O Level History. I'd studied Mussolini and the Spanish Civil War and the spread of fascism in Europe. And yet there had never been any mention (as far as I could recall) of Oswald Mosley and the British Union of Fascists. I had no idea that Hitler had many admirers – and close personal friends – amongst the British ruling classes, people who thought that fascism and dictatorship was preferable to democracy and socialism and would have welcomed it here.

As a child, I grew up in the shadow of the Second World War. I was of the generation whose parents and grandparents lived through it and had their own stories to tell. We were also deluged with books and films and television series set during the war. They all gave the impression that Britain had always seen the threat that Hitler posed and that the whole population had always been united against the Nazis. As a child, I swallowed the myth that plucky little Britain defeated Hitler and fascism all on its own.

As an adult, I began to realise that the reality was darker, uglier and a lot more complicated. I did, however, still firmly believe that we had learned the lessons of history. We had seen that fascism led directly from hate speech to the Holocaust. We would surely never be so cruel or so stupid as to go down that path again.

I never thought that in my lifetime I would see mainstream politicians stirring up hatred and division to gain power. And yet here we are.

As a writer, it seemed like the right time to think once more about the Battle of Cable Street. In writing this book, I want to celebrate the courage of the ordinary people who stood together on 4 October 1936. I want to remember that they won their fight. Because if they did that then, we can do it now and in the future.